Also available by the author: 'And Only the
Seagulls are Laughing.' Norman Setchell 2010
by Milton Contact.
ISBN 978-1-4908851-1-7

The Lost Family of Jesus

*Where Are the Descendants of the Brothers
and Sisters of Jesus of Nazareth?*

*Barbara Pye
&
William Fuessli*

WESTBOW
PRESS®
A DIVISION OF THOMAS NELSON
& ZONDERVAN

This is a work of fiction. All of the characters, names, incidents, organizations, and dialogue in this novel are either the products of the author's imagination or are used fictitiously.

WestBow Press books may be ordered through booksellers or by contacting:

WestBow Press
A Division of Thomas Nelson & Zondervan
1663 Liberty Drive
Bloomington, IN 47403
www.westbowpress.com
1 (866) 928-1240

ISBN: 978-1-4908-8511-7 (sc)

Library of Congress Control Number: 2015909810

Print information available on the last page.

WestBow Press rev. date: 08/04/2015

Contents

Dedication

This book is dedicated to our grandchildren, Elliot, Isaac, Imogen, Matthew and Molly; and to all young people who read this story about the life of Jesus.

In gratitude for the witness of so many women and men engaged in mission, and service to humanity, we promise to donate a percentage of any sales to the Mission Aviation Fellowship and The Sailors' Society.

"The Authors want to express their thanks to the team at Westbow Press for all their help and guidance."

Introduction

So little is known about the descendants of the brothers and sisters of Jesus of Nazareth. However, it is clear from the New Testament Gospel accounts that His mother, Mary had at least six other children with Joseph her husband. We know that Jesus had four brothers, James, Joseph, Jude and Simon, and also sisters, but there is no mention of how many or their names.

The factional stories you are about to read, you will find, are based on the Biblical accounts written in the Gospels, and are the imaginary accounts of one brother Joseph, and a younger sister, Talitha.

We are intrigued, as you may well be, with the thought that somewhere God Has provided a remnant of the descendants of Joseph and Mary, and that it is the intention of the authors to enhance our imagination of the life of Jesus Christ and the followers who were called to teach, heal and pass on the story of the fast growth of believers who suffered torture, imprisonment and, in many cases, execution for their faith in their Risen Lord and Saviour.

Although we have created an imaginative account spoken by a sister and brother, quotations from the Bible have been taken from The Living Bible, The New English Bible and Revised Standard Version.

Part One:
TALITHA'S STORY

TALITHA: Sister of Jesus

"Don't be frightened, Mary, for God has decided to bless you wonderfully! Very soon now you will become pregnant and have a baby boy, and you are to name him 'Jesus.' Luke 1 v 36.

He hugged me gently and kissed my forehead tenderly. I was aware of suppressed emotion but he turned and walked with firm resolute step through the small, low ceilinged, earth-floored room of our little home at the back of our father's workshop. The day was hot and humid but, nevertheless, I shivered uncontrollably. Then I turned and saw my little sister sobbing quietly in the corner comforted by our mother; such a calm, loving and God-fearing, reverent woman, just the dearest and most understanding mother any growing girl could be blessed with. She was, of course, hard-working – had to be with seven children to feed, clothe, guide and teach in the difficult times we were enduring under the cruel yoke of the Romans and the domination of the Pharisees and their countless pedantic man-made (although they would deny that) laws. Our five older brothers were now four at home since our beloved Yeshua, Yeshi to us all, had felt 'called' to hear our strange, wild-eyed cousin John preach and, he confided to us, to ask John to baptize him, for he knew his 'time had come' which puzzled us, but which our mother explained, meant he now felt ready to become the itinerant preacher God wanted. But Oh! I wanted to shout at him, "there are plenty of those already in our little country." We, God's special and chosen people, longed for His promised Messiah to come and rescue us. There had been some fervent false messiahs over the years with varying amounts of followers. Some had given up and run away, but some had felt the heavy hand of Rome and the leaders of our people.

Mother Mary, since our elderly father's demise, had begun to tell us beautiful tales of her young life, her betrothal to her dearly loved and respected Joseph. Joseph, our affectionate (but firm), but mostly monosyllabic and understandably calloused-handed 'Abba'. She told many enthralling stories, too, of God's goodness to her and her utter trust in Him, his guidance and protection for her when she could have been stoned to death for her pregnancy before God sent an angel to Joseph in a dream to reassure him of Mary's innocence and that he should marry her as soon as possible, which he immediately did! We didn't really understand this, nor her description of their journey to Bethlehem for the registration of all males from the line of King David, which Joseph was. Facts seemed to my sister and I to be mixed inseparably surely with mis-remembered things; but angels, she promised, had appeared to shepherds who came promptly to the stable where she had been forced to give birth as the only inn in the town was packed to capacity that night with others of David's line!

In the mercifully cool evenings after the heat of the days we listened to the sweet voice of the source of our whole security. We heard, amazingly, of three seers from distant lands, dressed richly and riding on camels with servants in tow, who arrived to see the new baby Jesus when he was a few days old and Mother, Father and the little one had moved, temporarily, to somewhere a little more comfortable. They left gifts too, knelt and seemed to be worshipping our brother! Mary said that in her youth and innocence she did not fully understand but kept these memories and pondered them, although she had been told that Jesus would, in due course, be the longed for Redeemer for Israel. This was affirmed by an elderly, highly respected, devout man named Simeon who was in the Temple in Jerusalem at the time Mary and Joseph travelled there to fulfil the law to offer their sacrifice for purification. He told them that the Lord had promised him that he would not die until he had seen God's anointed King and impelled by the Holy Spirit he had hurried to the Temple that day and when our parents arrived he took the baby into his arms, tears streaming down the ridges and wrinkles of his tired but serene old face. Mary and Joseph just marvelled at what he said next!

He said "Lord, I can now die content for your promise has come true and I have seen with my own poor eyes the Saviour you have given to the world. He will be the light for all nations and the glory of your people Israel!" But he added that Mary would know sorrow too "a sword shall pierce your soul, for this child will be rejected by many but will also be the great joy of many others."

Anna, too, a very old lady who lived in the Temple precincts, was there too praising and thanking God for this child.

The boys were sceptical of these woman's memories but were kind and considerate and respectful and listened with interest. Yeshi, we would later realize, but at the time were too young to fully comprehend, was profoundly moved and affected each time he heard any of these things since, of course, these stories were of HIS birth and also, later of their journey to Egypt to escape the horrors of King Herod's fear and fury. Again, a dream given to Joseph saved their lives as an angel told him to leave at once, in the middle of the night and go to Egypt and await further instructions!

Our dear brother had eyes which seemed to be very frequently moist with unshed tears and these eyes were so observant of all around, so able, it seemed, to know our thoughts and to then understand even the simple feelings of my feisty little sister, Susannah, and myself; we knew he loved us unconditionally despite our silliness and inane giggling. We saw, too, his sense of responsibility to, after Joseph's death, train up his younger brothers, or at least encourage them to become excellent carpenters, in order to earn the keep for the family when he departed on his 'calling' and so that they might marry and in God's time have families of their own. Despite Mother's efforts Yeshi was adamant that he could not marry as he must devote himself, body, mind and spirit to fulfilling God's plan for his life. Well, as can be imagined, this was a great disappointment to local young women and their mothers! For who could not love such a kind, respectful man filled with love of God and his neighbours; loyal to his family and even a carpenter as good, if not surpassing, the skills of Joseph. His yokes for farmers' oxen were known for their comfort for the poor beasts and their lightness. No-one could understand how he achieved this but when money was available after good harvests the orders came in for them.

Later on he said that HIS yokes were easy and his burdens light with a meaning which some understood, but others needed to have explained to them, including me, that 'yoke' was the name given to any Rabbi's interpretation of the Scriptures and some interpretations were 'heavy' indeed and a burden to the lives of the people in their particular care. Yeshi's teachings were 'light' because he wanted people to just put their trust in him and look to God for their care and sustenance and to obey God and not the petty teachings which became burdens, of some Pharisees and Rabbis.

Always those eyes seemed truly the windows to his soul and looked upon all he met with understanding and compassion, even those who mistrusted him and wanted his ministry ended. I knew that he prayed for their change of heart and mind and hoped they would come to know God better, as a God of infinite love and mercy in the way which he himself did...

Then Jesus went from his home in Galilee to the river Jordan to be baptized there by John. Matthew ch 3. v 13

The favourite game for Susie and myself when we had finished our household chores was 'Mothers and Babies' with the wooden dolls our Abba/Papa had carved for us from sweet-smelling pomegranate wood and clothed by Mother from scraps of clothe left over from the special seamless cloak she had woven and sewn for Yeshi before his departure from us. We squabbled a little over who should put their baby in the manger/bed left in the workshop because the farmer who had ordered it had died and his widow was forced by inevitable poverty to move away to live with family. This happened unsurprisingly because she was bullied into selling up at a fraction of the true value of the land, to the son of a synagogue leader from Jerusalem. I expect such things go on everywhere! We 'borrowed' a little straw from our donkey's shelter and laid an old clothe for each baby's head, which reminded us, of course, of Yeshua's own birth story.

We heard from a friend that Yeshi had, indeed, been baptized, as many others also had been, but his was special in that at the moment of his rising from the water a white dove landed on his shoulder and, this friend was sure, a voice from heaven said "you are my much loved Son, yes, my delight." But, this friend also told us, some just thought it thundered but he HEARD, as did both John and Yeshua!

No-one seemed to know where he disappeared to after that until he told later of his being led, he said, into the desert for a long time; he lost count of the number of days but was told he had been gone for forty days! How could anyone survive for forty days without food or especially water? I have learned recently, from one of the disciples of our dear one, that he eventually confided his terrible fears whilst there and temptations to give up on his calling, of the hallucinations, the unbearable heat and bone-chilling night-time cold, of the black thoughts and the tangible presence of evil. But, he told, too, of knowing God's Holy Presence and of angels sustaining and strengthening him through that agonising time. He told also of the desert animals lying near him at night so that they warmed each other; even God's creatures felt Yeshi's loving, compassionate nature and showed no fear of him but, indeed, wanted to be near him. That, as much as anything at the time made me weep, for I have, myself, such empathy with animals for they, too, struggle to survive and often endure hunger, thirst and worst of all the cruelty of men. I have seen so many donkeys neglected and beaten, with ribs showing through lack of nourishment and hooves curling because no-one has cared enough to trim them, and with sores that the hot weather and flies refuse to allow to heal. Yet still, they struggle on, overloaded and abused; you would think their owners would have enough sense, let alone compassion, to treat them well as they work so hard for them and how would men manage without them for transport of themselves and their goods to market. I didn't know at that time that such a humble little beast would be the chosen means of taking Yeshi into Jerusalem at his and God's right and chosen time.

Jesus stretched out his hand and touched him.   Luke 5.v 17

Time and again we were stunned by the reports that reached us in our little Nazareth of our brother's ministry; this was far, far more than the life of just a travelling preacher and teacher. We learned of a leper he TOUCHED! Surely, we thought, and hoped, this could not be true! We were anxious for him for this reason but as time went on and despite his reassurances to us on his all too rare visits home, we became more so since we knew his popularity with our people was increasing and the jealousy and indeed fury of the Pharisees was ill-concealed.

I, Talitha, at fourteen and now a woman fell wonderfully and disturbingly in love with John, not cousin John, but young John, a dear friend and faithful follower of Yeshi. John worshipped Yeshi as his mentor and example of all a man could be, and I loved John for loving my beautiful big brother so much. John visited us on these rare occasions with Yeshi and various other of his 'disciples'/friends over the period of the next two years or so. They ate with us and slept out in our yard under that wonderful canopy of God's creation, the millions of stars, beneath our fig and pomegranate trees. We knew that God had promised our ancestor Abraham that his descendents would be as numerous as the stars in the heavens and now, indeed, the Jewish people were very numerous but we suffered as we seemed to have always done according to the Torah's record of our history and movements; still we were under the heavy yoke of the Pharisees and the Romans and wondered if God would ever send his promised Messiah to free us and ease our spirits and bodies of their pains. Added to which drought and the pestilence of locusts too, which seemed to come our way every few years, kept us struggling. We all struggled but got on with the practicalities of survival but Yeshi spent more and more of his time, after his days work at the carpenter's bench, building up to the time of his leaving us, out in the hills, all night sometimes. Very few people during these times of austerity could afford new yokes for their oxen, even though Yeshi's yokes were known afar for their comfort for the poor beasts and their relative lightness compared to some which they had to endure, which rubbed and made them fractious and infected badly, sometimes. People could not even afford to have broken tables and chairs mended but as these are essential parts of a home, our Yeshi would often mend them where necessary and just say to pay him when they could, knowing, of course, that they probably would never have even a few small coins to spare for that!

We could only guess, of course, but because of his gentle nature and his deep love of the family and the people, we knew he would be praying when he disappeared into the night, beseeching God to guide him, to help the people and to show him His Way and Will for his life and work, so we did not worry too much about his safety on these more and more frequent occasions.

Meanwhile, I longed for John, himself then only seventeen, to notice me but he hardly spoke to me, but when he did give me a big grin, I felt so special, but on the whole I'm sure he just saw me as a little girl, well-trained in domesticity! His mind, rightly so, was on his friendship with Yeshi and all he could learn from him and all he might be able to do to help him.

As Yeshi's travels continued we heard from those who had gone out to hear him, or from strangers passing through Nazareth who were welcomed and fed by Mother, of many compassionate, hardly believable, one can only call miracles which Jesus (as some called him – meaning Saviour, which certainly puzzled me) was able to do with God's power and mercy. The wonderful stories of the blind seeing again, or even seeing for the first time, having been born blind! Of the lame leaping with the joy of strengthened legs, and deaf and dumb shouting aloud and never stopping their chattering when their ears were unblocked and their tongues loosened. Oh! The joy and astonishment that filled our hearts! We learned of an elderly woman who was cured after twelve years of bleeding which no doctor could stop; twelve years, how my young mind sympathised for I dreaded those four-weekly aches and cramps in my belly and feeling unable to cope with the embarrassment of being a woman. Mother was understanding and kind, allowing me to rest from my chores when things got too uncomfortable, but, of course, I was 'unclean' by the law and therefore unable to serve anyone with their food. She would make me a warm drink of milk from our goat and heat a stone in the oven and wrap it in a clothe to hug to my stomach! It was said that this poor, ostracised and lonely woman just touched the edge of his garment as he was on his way, with the usual crowd around, pushing and trying to get nearer to him, with Jairus, a synagogue official, to his home because his little girl of twelve years was near death.

Jairus in his deep desperation and despite his doubts about the miracles, had begged Jesus to come and heal his daughter. So the delay when Jesus stopped to speak to the rejoicing but humble and grateful woman must have been unbearably frustrating for Jairus. Jesus, on his arrival, turned away the mourners, some of whom were genuine of course, but some were 'professional' mourners; Jesus wouldn't allow anyone into the little girl's room except Peter, James and young John and the parents of the child. He told everyone that she was not dead, but sleeping, although the mourners laughed at this statement because they 'knew' she was dead. When he stepped into the dimly lit room and saw the pale face of the child and felt the heartbreak of the parents his own heart filled with that ache that compassion brings; he took her by the hand and tenderly said "Talitha cumi" that is "little darling," (or more literally, little gazelle) "get up!" (I have wondered ever since if he chose my name, Talitha, when I was a baby, since all babies are 'little darlings!'). Anyway, she opened her eyes and a little colour returned to her puzzled face, after a moment or two she sat up and her parents were overcome with happiness, amazed and so grateful, of course. He said to wipe their tears of joy, stop hugging their fragile wraith-child and give her something to eat. I have wondered since hearing of this if she was perhaps afflicted with that disease of a few girls coming up to womanhood of losing their appetite and somehow wishing to stay a child and avoid the advancing years into adulthood and soon to be matrimony and the responsibilities seen to be part of that; I have known at least one girl in our own village who refused to eat or drink and eventually passed away despite all efforts to save her. Anyway, by this time the little girl's mother had fainted! From joy or shock we don't know! But Jesus also asked everyone present not to tell anyone the details of this healing; a difficult request to keep to! Ever after Jairus was brave enough, together with his friend Nicodemus, to be followers of Jesus, albeit secretly, in fear of the Leaders of our people.

We learned soon after that his band of twelve followers had increased as Jesus had chosen up to seventy to help him spread the good news of the coming of God's Kingdom.

Whose wife will she be?   Matthew Ch 22

Many times the Pharisees and Sadducees tried to trick Yeshi into saying something which would bring him before the Sanhedrin, for they feared for their jobs, affluent way of life and indeed their very lives if the Romans decided Yeshi's work constituted a threat to their rule. With much pleading I eventually persuaded James and Jude to take me along to hear our brother speak. I felt a little sibling triumph as Simon, one year my senior, wanted to go too, but must stay home to look after the rest of the family, as Joseph the next in line, in age, to Yeshi was already away from home working at his trade in the home of a wealthy Pharisee. I was so eager to go with James and Jude just to be amongst the vast crowd of thousands, but without the knowledge of our presence for Yeshi. On this particular occasion he was asked by a Sadducee even though they have no belief in resurrection or heaven, whose wife a woman would be in heaven if she had had seven husbands, all brothers, who had each died. Well Yeshi was undeterred by the facetiousness of this question and quietly answered that the dead do not marry but in that respect are like the angels. We were surprised at the clarity of his voice which carried over such a large area as he certainly did not raise it purposely. He seemed to understand the terrain and the kind of area at which to place himself for that purpose. On this occasion he seemed to sense that we were there for he looked at length towards where we were but we could not read in his face whether that would please him or not. Being the child I was I wanted to wave! I was restrained!

He continued to upbraid the Sadducees accusing them of ignorance of the Scriptures! We feared his righteous anger would get him into trouble as again he called the Herodians, a Jewish political party, hypocrites! This occurred on the same day also when they asked, at the behest of the Pharisees, if it was right to pay taxes to the Roman Government or not. The crowd loved Jesus' reply

"Show me a coin. Whose picture is stamped on it and whose name is this beneath the picture?

Well, of course, they had to reply that it was Caesar's.

"Well then" he said "give it to Caesar if it is Caesar's but give God everything that belongs to God."

They were surprised, baffled and no doubt furious, but the crowd were very impressed by his answers, especially when in tender loving tones as to those who were, indeed, poor, hurting and in many, many, cases in despair he said

"You would think these Pharisees were Moses the way they keep making up so many laws, which they expect you to keep, loading you with petty demands which they themselves do not even try to keep. Everything they do is for show."

Jesus spoke at length with bravery and determination on this subject near to the hearts of the populace. He warned the Pharisees in no uncertain terms about pretending to be holy by their showy behaviour, their love of the deference of others and even accusing them of being like beautiful mausoleums – full of dead men's bones and of foulness and corruption. After many times calling them hypocrites he seemed to cry in exasperation, frustration and exhaustion -

"Oh! Jerusalem, Jerusalem, the city that kills the prophets. How often I have wanted to gather your children together as a hen gathers her chicks beneath her wings, but you wouldn't let me!"

Well, James, Jude and I tried hurriedly to get to his side to comfort him and move him away but he slipped through the vast throng with his disciples a protective shield around him and so, reluctantly and full of anxiety and foreboding, we began our return journey to Nazareth. On our arrival and although they were eager to know everything Yeshi had said and done we told our mother and young Susannah and Simon little of all we had seen and heard and nothing of our fears. We reassured them that he was loved by the ordinary people and he had said they were like sheep, lost and frightened but that he is their shepherd. He was so full of kindness and compassion, understanding of the human condition, so able to explain to simple folk things they needed to know about the coming Kingdom of God. Who could not love this special, God-inspired man? Who would want his death? This was the whisper we heard. James and Jude voiced their thoughts quietly so, as they thought, the rest of us would not hear, that they were not sure that he wasn't losing his mind. It so upset Mother that she and the boys tried to bring him home on one occasion at least for a long rest to recover from his exhaustion and to be out of the focus of those determined to put an end to his work amongst the poor and needy. He would have none of it and even stated forcefully to those around that anyone who obeys God in Heaven, his Father, is his brother and sister and mother! To our surprise Mother was not hurt or upset by this remark but seemed to understand this and others of his sayings to the people.

We heard of the wonderful tales he told using examples of everyday happenings of farmers sowing seed, of prodigal sons returning home and of women sweeping their home or baking bread, all to illustrate the coming Kingdom he spoke of. Many, including us, were puzzled by some things, but even amused by and heartened and, indeed, instructed, by others. Mother understood better than her children that Jesus' power was from God, that he said or did nothing unless his Heavenly Father wanted it so; she knew his strength was from God alone but she worried even so. One day I heard her praying one of the Psalms, saying "O my God, blow away his enemies like dust; like chaff before the wind. Utterly disgrace them until they recognize your power and your name, O

Lord God. Bend down and hear my prayer, O Lord, and answer me."

Of course, I crept away without disturbing her.

Yeshi's sense of humour even surfaced occasionally which was not something he was really known for, being serious and thoughtful from childhood. But that little tale of a camel passing through the eye of a needle, the name for one of the very narrow gates of Jerusalem, made many smile, as they had often seen rich merchants pushing and goading their poor beasts to squeeze through or even having to take the trouble to unload them! Jesus said to his disciples, as he watched this little drama one day, that it would be that difficult for a rich man to enter Heaven! We heard of a very rich and well known young man who turned down the opportunity to follow Jesus because he could not bring himself to give away his money and property. Yeshi asked him to do this because he knew this young man and that he was law-abiding but he knew also he needed to stop making money his idol and to be near to himself to learn of true riches.

Jesus speaks on the Mount

Perhaps the most memorable but puzzling talks to his disciples (although we and others were able to overhear) was, as the usual vast throng of young, old and sick were gathering. He sat, which indicated the import, in the tradition of Rabbis, of all he was about to say. He said slowly, thoughtfully, as if listening and waiting for God's voice of approval before he spoke each 'blessing.' He even said that those who mourn are blessed. Did I really hear that, for how could anyone who had lost a loved one be blessed? But he said that they would be comforted and he meant, I understand, that they would have God's loving Presence near them and their relatives and friends would also attempt to comfort them in all the ways of tradition and kindness – with food, with child-minding, with tending their livestock or harvesting their fields – anything that in the period of mourning was impossible to undertake. Other things he said on that day were hard, such as "blessed are those who long for justice, for they shall surely have it." How our people longed for justice and also "blessed are the kind and merciful for they shall be shown mercy." From all around we heard of the hardness of our conquerors towards ordinary citizens, themselves mostly kind people, who were certainly shown no mercy or kindness from the Romans and precious little from our leaders. He spoke at great length that day of persecution for those who follow him, and later of Moses and the prophets, of divorce, of not making vows and – a profound shock to the ears of all – "Love your enemies!"

The mass intake of breath at this was audible and for a moment we thought the crowd might turn against him but big Peter jumped up, looking fiercely around from under his dark shaggy brows and the crowd quietened, to our great relief. Yeshi continued to teach and heal for several hours. The people always seemed amazed at his teaching for he taught as one who had great authority and did not just discuss the writings and thoughts and beliefs of well-known Rabbis, past or present.

"For I was hungry and you fed me; I was thirsty and you gave me water; I was a stranger and you invited me into your homes; naked and you clothed me; sick and in prison and you visited me."
Matthew chapter 25 v. 35

Jesus, more than once, reiterated that we all, however in want ourselves, should certainly share what food we have with those who have none; if anyone is without adequate clothes we must give some of ours; any stranger tired, hungry and with nowhere to lay their head must be made welcome in our homes and we should visit the lonely and frightened in prison and, of course, care for the sick. For he said that if we refused to do these things we were, in fact, refusing to help him! He said our eternal life depends on how we treat others for it is himself we help or turn away from! Our eternal life depends, too, on the belief we should have that he was sent by God to bring forgiveness and salvation to all who would trust in him, the Son of Man, as he often called himself, although others wanted to call him and indeed make him their king!

This pronouncement was very thought provoking, but he called his disciples and those who wanted to follow him other mystifying names :- "Salt of the earth" and "A Light on a Hill which mustn't be Hidden." He often quoted the Psalms of King David and said that he, himself, would be their fulfilment, but we failed to understand, as did even his disciples, who were chosen by him to learn from him and do the works he was able to do with God's help and even greater things. Well, THAT was unbelievable! "I will instruct you" he promised "and teach you and counsel you" even as God had promised David in those olden days we learned about at synagogue from our own elderly, frail Rabbi. Scripture also told us that Yahweh had promised his people a cornerstone in Zion, "chosen and precious, and the one who trusts in him will never be put to shame."

Well, I know I am only a woman, of less importance than any man, but I was eager to learn all that God had taught and promised and I seemed to learn as much from Mother, indeed, as from our Rabbi who refused to teach girls as was the custom and tradition but doted on his cleverer boys who were quick to learn. I had the notion that he had hoped that Yeshi would take his place eventually as the Rabbi for Nazareth. Yeshi had been his pupil for a short time and always listened avidly, politely, but also asked questions which, maybe, shocked Rabbi Ben-Simeon who once irritably accused him of learning too much for his age on the occasion he spent three days questioning the Pharisees in Jerusalem when he was able to visit with our parents soon after his twelfth birthday. (This was before I was born!) They returned from that journey subdued and thoughtful and Jesus apologised again for worrying them by 'disappearing' for three days but he had assumed they would know he must be in "his Father's House." However, we were told he was obedient to Mary and Joseph after that and was well-loved by all who knew him.

At this point I will digress a little to tell of Mother's dearest friend, Dorcas, and of her skills with the loom and needle. She was a wonderful example of someone who constantly kept the needs of others on her mind. The garments she made and decorated with tiny flower motives were exquisite and given away to any in need! I must just add that really and truly we were not supposed to decorate things, except that the Pharisees had elaborate garments decorated with embroidered pomegranates for wearing at special feasts, while many of the very poor shivered at night under the moon or were burned by the hot sun by day because of the inadequacy of their garments. Well Dorcas spend most of her time sewing so her patch of land was not very productive, but she enjoyed the fruits of the season nevertheless since the recipients of her generosity made sure she had sufficient of everything available and, her few chickens scratched around for anything available and gave her enough eggs!

This reminds me that Jesus urged people not to worry about whether they had enough to eat or clothes for their backs as life consists of far more than food or raiment. And he said worrying won't add a single day to anyone's life! But he said that he is Life and anyone coming to him would never thirst! His sayings were beautiful and touched deeply the spiritual parts of people and made them long for this Kingdom of God he spoke about all the time. "The Kingdom of God is within you" – did he mean within each individual or within the community? Or both? He spoke of the Kingdom coming but already here! He stressed not to worry but keep our minds on this Kingdom he talked of so lovingly. He used a beautiful example, I remember hearing, of the lilies of the fields, saying that even King Solomon in all his glory was not as exquisitely arrayed as these lilies for nothing could surpass their colour and texture and what a wonderful Creator God we have.

"Our heavenly Abba," he called out to the great throng assembled around him with eager faces, "knows the needs of all his children and will provide from day to day, as He did for our ancestors in the desert for forty years as Moses led them from captivity as slaves in Egypt to the Promised Land." This would be if only we would all make the Kingdom of God our primary concern.

As a young girl I did not understand the meaning but loved the beauty of the words from this brave brother of mine; a person, himself, of great inner beauty of character I knew. I suspected this may have been the case for some of the people present too.

He raised the ire of many synagogue leaders by healing on the Sabbath day. Our Jewish people, young and old, grew up believing that illness and disease were punishments from Yahweh for their sins or the sins of their parents or back two or three generations, but Yeshi, because of his closeness to God, his constant contact with him through prayer, knew this was so wrong, just superstition to give some explanation to illness or deformity or blindness and so on. He said emphatically many times illness is not God's wish for his beloved ones, nor disability, but these things come from the evil which abounds in the world and is part of that evil. Not God's will; God's will within His Kingdom is love, joy, peace, forgiveness one to another. These things are hard to believe when in pain or seeing a loved one unable to live normally. I saw with my own eyes his healing of an old lady who was bent double, she whispered, "for the last eighteen years, Teacher." On another Sabbath occasion he looked around angrily at the Pharisees because he could hardly believe their complete lack of compassion for the sick. On this particular day he gave a man with a withered arm its full use back again.

"Would you not rescue an animal which had fallen into a pit on the Sabbath?" he asked the Pharisees.

Many months passed peaceably enough in Nazareth and we continued to hear about our loved one's journeys and miraculous healings and also that he became even more firm and resolute in all he undertook; he was now thin, but probably fit too, because he and his followers walked many miles from town to town, sometimes staying a few days and always welcomed by the common folk and watched by the employees of our leaders for any slips or blasphemies.

We were not, ourselves, present, since Jerusalem is about three days walk from Nazareth – if you are young and strong – so we heard only of Yeshi borrowing an unbroken donkey and riding it into Jerusalem. His purpose only later becoming clear, but we wondered at the gentle touch and soothing words he must have had in order to calm the beast as the people shouted and threw palm leaves and coats down for it to walk on, in welcome to Jesus.

They called out "God has given us a king!" They were exultant "Glory to God" they cried. But, did they understand that their Jesus was trying to show them that he came as their servant and saviour, if only they would believe in him and God's Kingdom and follow his teachings, not as any sort of conqueror. Young and old were overjoyed at this procession but were to be disappointed if they imagined he was about to gather their young men together to overthrow Rome!

On seeing the city ahead he wept, although only the disciples walking by the side of him noticed, of course. He said, as if to himself

"Your enemies are going to crush you Jerusalem, because you have rejected the person and the opportunity to repent and change which Yahweh has offered you."

When he reached the Temple he seemed to break under the additional strain of seeing God's House so misused; he made a rope and drove out the animals and the merchants; these animals were being sold at exorbitant prices for the sacrifices and sold as animals without blemish when it was abundantly clear they were not always perfect! Many people made lots of money fraudulently from these sales to people who could ill-afford their prices, but felt it their duty to have the best for the sacrifices, to assuage their guilt, maybe. Tradition anyway. The money-changers fared no better for they, too, were corrupt. Jesus quoted Scripture saying

"My Temple is a place of prayer; but you have turned it into a den of thieves."

I knew, when I learned of this, that the Pharisees would not, could not, overlook this! I felt almost paralysed with fear for Yeshi for I knew he had gone too far, this time.

So it proved for a few weeks later our Beloved was taken whilst at prayer, as was his habit, at the Mount of Olives, betrayed, it turned out, by Judas Iscariot, one who had eaten with him, listened to him, walked and talked with him, been we thought a faithful friend. Why? Why would he do such a thing? Greed? He held the purse for the group. Was it disappointment that Jesus was not, after all, going to free the people from their dictators? Was not going to lead an uprising to overthrow Rome? Or did he believe that right until the last minute that Jesus would in some supernatural way show his power and the people's longings for freedom would somehow be accomplished?

Whatever was in his disturbed mind after Jesus' death he committed what was seen as one of the greatest sins and hanged himself.

Yeshi's trial, or trials more accurately, were farcical and even Pontius Pilot wanted to release him but certain loud voices in the crowds bribed by, threatened and frightened by the leaders, screamed for his death and the release of Barabbas, even though he was a notorious rebel and murderer of Roman soldiers. I cannot to this day believe that all those present who had hung on his every word and received their loved ones back from crippling illness did that, but were outnumbered and out-shouted.

Dear Mary Magdalene, that sweet, reformed, loving woman, my John and Mother were the only ones of Jesus family or friends brave enough to risk arrest themselves and were nearby during Yeshi's physical and mental torment. He gave Mother into John's care and John into Mother's care. Also, and this is breathtaking, he forgave those who were killing him; he asked God to forgive them "for they don't know what they are doing."

Our normally calm and reasonable Mother was not in her right mind for many days afterward, but rocked and slept, moaned and wouldn't eat; everyone was thankful that she slept a great deal, but nonetheless fitfully. She later, much later, told us that her beloved first-born had promised one of the criminals crucified alongside himself, that he would be with Yeshi, that day, in Paradise! What comfort, what absolute love for another whilst in his own agonies.

"As the crowd led Jesus away to his death, Simon of Cyrene, who was just coming into Jerusalem from the country, was forced to follow, carrying Jesus' cross. Great crowds trailed behind, and many grief-stricken women." Luke 23. V 26/27

As Jesus attempted to carry the cross-beam along the Via Dolorosa he fell more than once through loss of blood and pain and exhaustion; the Romans supervising this pulled a strong looking man out of the crowd to carry this for Jesus, since he would not have made it to Golgotha. The sympathetic quietness of the crowd was broken only by the sobbing of women, one of whom wiped Jesus brow with her scarf until she was pushed roughly away, another poured a little water into his bruised and bleeding mouth and each was rewarded with a look of grateful love.

Simon of Cyrene was the person to whom fell this unenviable task; he heaved this heavy burden onto his strong back, breaking into a groan and great drops of sweat even though only also in his thirties and therefore about the same age as Jesus, but stocky and muscular.

When this unhappy journey was complete and Simon turned to go away, having no wish to see this torment, oft repeated by the Romans, his breath felt knocked from his body and his legs felt like water because the bruised and abused face which gave him a thankful look was non other than the man who, two years previously, had driven demons and madness from him. Simon at that time was an insane young man and had been since childhood, whose life had become unbearable and who lived among the tombstones on the lakeside, cutting himself with sharp stones in attempts to relieve his mental torment and drive the horrific pictures from his mind. This wonderful man now in agony himself had made him well and whole again and, he believed, had driven all the demons from him into a herd of pigs which then panicked and stampeded into the lake. This wonderful healer and man of God had understood his ranting and raving and the fact that he could only keep repeating "Legion." Jesus had calmed him, touched him (the first person for so long) and told him that he would now be better. Simon had, when in his right mind again and his nakedness clothed by the generous gift of a mantel from one of the followers of this wonderful person, told Jesus that as a little boy of about four he had witnessed the slaughter, at King Herod's command, of all the baby boys under two years old, by the Legions of Roman soldiers; his own baby brother was among them. Healing tears were shed, by himself, but Jesus wept too and his disciples with him, because Jesus knew that his birth had triggered this monstrous obscenity. After a little time spent together Simon had wanted to be a follower of Jesus and begged to go with him, but Jesus had replied that he must go back to his family now living in Cyrene and tell them of the wonderful thing that God has done for him.

Simon's wish to follow Jesus was fulfilled in the rest of his life; he never ceased at every opportunity to tell anyone who would listen of the wonderful thing Jesus had done for him.

His Resurrection

Our hearts bursting, almost stopping with the joy, astonishment, disbelief of such a miracle, we saw our dear one risen from death, resurrected, returned to us from that garden tomb. Mary Magdalene was the first to have that heart-stopping moment in the Garden of Gethsemane, as through her tears she asked who she assumed was the gardener, where Yeshi's body had been taken, as the tomb was empty on the morning after the Sabbath which was the third day after his death. Oh! Her joy to hear him say her **name**. She ran to embrace him but he gently told her she must not touch him "as he had not yet ascended to his Father." She eventually reluctantly left him to run to the disciples to tell them the astounding news.

They were locked away safely in the same upper room where their Teacher had shared his Last Supper with them, washing their feet, as a servant to show them they must serve each other and their neighbour and saying that he would shed his blood and his body be broken, as the bread they were eating, for sinners, for their redemption and forgiveness and everlasting life. Not understood at the time, I believe, by anyone! Anyway, as Mary arrived and knocked hard on the door, they hesitated to open, naturally, but she persisted and shouted out that it was only herself and eventually she was able to say what had happened in the Garden. It was impossible to believe and I think the disciples thought she was hysterical with grief. However, eventually Peter and John ran to the tomb. My John, being younger and fitter, since Peter was quite a bulky man, outran Peter, but Peter being bolder went into the tomb first and then John. What they saw confirmed Mary's story for the cloth in which Jesus had been wrapped by Joseph of Arimathea and the helpers, whose newly created tomb this was, was lying there and the head bandage lying separately. It had taken several strong men to take down Yeshi from that cross and carry him to the tomb although several of the women who had been standing a long way off, followed at a distance and saw where he had been laid.

Much later, and it even took more explanations from our Saviour during his forty days with us before his Ascension to His Father (and our Father), it slowly dawned upon us and our minds were at last opened to the truth that our brother, son, friend, teacher was, indeed, the promised Messiah. Words only fail to express adequately our overwhelming gratitude, love and encouragement. Why had we been so slow to understand and believe? For many Scriptural prophesies were fulfilled in his life, ministry, death and resurrection.

Even I an uneducated young woman, knew that the Psalms spoke of the Messiah ministering to the poor and needy, that he would teach in parables, of miracles and his rejection. His betrayal by a friend was foretold and even his being sold for thirty pieces of silver. Isaiah told us that he would be silent before his accusers (which he was) and that he would be beaten and spat upon. One of the Psalms even speaks of his being offered wine vinegar in his suffering. Other prophecies, so numerous, and so fulfilled foretold that his bones would not be broken but his side would be pierced and of his burial in a rich man's grave. Even the disciples' appointment of a successor to Judas was spoken of in a Psalm. His resurrection, ascension the Psalms foretell. All this detail is not coincidence! Our God, our Yahweh, planned this way of Redemption for his fallen and sinful children, because he loves us so much that he gave us his Son, born of the Holy Spirit with Mary.

He is Messiah and Redeemer not just for the Jewish people but for the Gentiles too and for all the world and all the ages to come, until his promised return.

**"All the believers were of one heart and mind .....
And the apostles preached powerful sermons
about the Resurrection of the Lord Jesus."** Acts
ch 4 v 32/33

John, indeed, cared for Mother, with my help, since we married some two years later when I was nineteen years old (quite an old unmarried woman by our traditions, since fifteen was not at all unusual). Mother was this age when she married Father and just a girl, but obedient to God's will for her life and even rejoiced that he should use her, just an ordinary (but pious) girl, a pure maid, for the conception, nurture and raising of His promised Messiah.

We lived in Nazareth in great simplicity whilst saving all we could as it was our hope and, we felt, calling, to go abroad to take the Good News to others far away. We even thought we would tell rich people the Good News, if given the chance, as they, too, needed saving!

During this time our Susannah became betrothed to and a year later married a neighbour. The only one of us to then stay in Nazareth. This wedding, a little more lavish than that of John and myself, and as indeed did each wedding, reminded us of the Wedding in Cana of a distant relative about eight years previously. But it seemed so much longer ago because of the work, death and resurrection of Jesus in that time; a ministry of just three years yet so much achieved by him in healing and teaching. Yet all seemed to have become a failure when he was taken by his enemies but he has triumphed over death and has promised eternal life to all who will believe in him, the Son of Man, which was his favourite name for himself, sent from God and now returned to his heavenly home, where he has promised to prepare places for us and fetch us to be with him when our time comes. Oh! He fills my heart and mind now!

At this wedding we were told Yeshi was able, reluctantly at first, it seemed, to perform his first miracle; done to save great embarrassment to the host and bridegroom as the supply of wine had run out. Well, I thought when I heard this, what greedy guests as always there is plenty for celebrations to go on sometimes for several days! Until everyone is exhausted I suppose and just want to go home. The cost and work involved in the catering, done by the women of the two families, is always staggering. How hard we women have to work and sometimes, I admit, even though I am young and healthy, I feel very tired! Well, on this happy occasion and everyone was happy (!!), Yeshi, with Yahweh's great mercy and understanding and we believe and suppose joy at the joining of this dear young couple, was able to change water into wine! Huge amounts of it too! Jugs and jugs! He explained later that wine does come from water – the rain sent from Yahweh, with the soil's nourishment too enables the grapes to grow for harvesting in the fullness of time and produces wine to cheer us, especially at weddings! He prayed that Yahweh would, supernaturally, and in his great mercy and love, speed up the process! Well, doesn't that just fill you with wonder and awe? Mother Mary seemed to understand that Yeshi could do this although, as I said, he was reluctant and said his time for miracles was not yet. But, he prayed about this and felt compelled to do his Father's bidding to save sadness and shock to the two families if everyone had to leave too early. Did Yeshi really believe this change could truly happen? Was he as surprised as the steward who tasted it and declared it better than anything else they had drunk and why had the best been kept until last?

John, Mother and I eventually made our way to the coastal port of Tyre and having saved long and hard for the fares, took ship to Ephesus where we were met and taken care of by our Brothers and Sisters of The Way, as they were called. Eunice and Lois especially were very kind and hospitable to us for a long time until we were able to rent our own little home because John was able to find work and Mother, like Dorcas, began to sew and sell garments to the local people. Mother became, over time, well-loved and respected by, particularly, the women of the town, because of her good listening ear and ability to empathise and offer prayers and comfort for anyone in distress. Her humility remained absolute despite some wanting to give her great praise for being the mother of Jesus! She always said that we and they must worship only, Father, Son and the Holy Spirit who is our comforter and guide, whom Jesus had promised to send to all who believe in him and that he, Jesus, was sent by the Father to be the world's one and only Saviour.

Some of my brothers had married by this time but remained in grave danger of arrest for, without exception, were all of the faith. Our, previously sceptical, James became leader of the church in Jerusalem and to our heartbreak and sorrow was killed some years later, leaving a wife and my two small nieces. They were sustained and comforted by all the believers in Jerusalem and the believers here made a collection for them which was sent by a Brother courier together with letters from us and our hopes that they would come to live with us here. However, as they were so loved in Jerusalem and his wife needed for His work within that community that did not happen.

Saul of Tarsus, that greatly feared persecutor of Believers in Jesus having been dramatically converted by the appearance of the Lord Jesus whilst on his way to Damascus then called himself an Apostle of Christ Jesus and became a tireless, endlessly brave preacher of the Good News of Christ risen. He thanked God endlessly for the strength for this, despite some physical weaknesses and diminishing eyesight, caused in part by the beatings and deprivation he had stoically endured; the many instances of brutal treatment for preaching the Word. He daily said that he was the worst of sinners, having persecuted and insulted Jesus, but that Jesus came into the world to save sinners.

Timothy, the son and grandson of Eunice and Lois received communications from Paul, as he now was, setting out advice for the running of the church here and the desired character of chosen leaders and the conduct of women, who, he urged, should be modest in their dress and rich in good deeds and not in gold or fancy dresses! Personally I thought this a bit presumptuous of him, but dared not say so, of course. He was not a married man so perhaps did not understand women too well! Anyway, none of the women I knew to be believers would dream of dressing immodestly and we certainly didn't have money for gold ornamentation!

He wrote that he hoped to come and see us all soon and in the meantime Timothy was not to let anyone look down on him because he was young! The letters were read to us to our great encouragement as, unsurprisingly I suppose, some had began to slip away. His wise words to us were of great help and I forgave him for not understanding women!

Yeshi, although also, of course, unmarried had understood women (perhaps partly due to having us two sisters!) but all his life treated women with great respect almost bordering on deference but with gentleness even when dealing with irritable old ladies in pain. That Mary Magdalene had the immense privilege of being the first of anyone to meet him after his resurrection is astounding as one would have thought the apostles would have been in that position. So many times the natural tenderness in his voice towards us and his mother was so helpful and reassuring when difficult circumstances brought us to the verge of tears, even in severe drought or the news that Roman soldiers were nearing our village or at the death of a near and dear friend and neighbour.

Always he urged us to trust in Father God for all we needed and talk to God and tell Him our fears and not forget to thank Him for all that He had done for us in the past and was constantly doing. I try to remember this and recall his lovely voice and the dear, familiar 'country' accent he had and laughingly exaggerated sometimes, especially to strangers passing through. Occasionally a little light mischief would be seen in this gentle way and he knew this made us all smile and we would join in the joke.

Eventually, Paul was able to visit us in Ephesus and despite all that he had suffered was with great passion and wonderful rhetoric able to bring many to the knowledge, love and service of Jesus and to bring back from slipping away a good many too! I changed my view of him once I had met this very ordinary looking little man and heard him speak for, most certainly, he was God inspired and had the deepest love for Yeshi, my brother, whom I know knew with God-given certainty was the promised Anointed One of God.

Paul would not stay long, despite our pleadings but continued on his travels; we heard of shipwrecks and more beatings over the years but always he wanted us and all the churches he apparently corresponded with to live in agreement with each other and in peace; always for the building up of faith in each dear child of the Father and believer in our Messiah, the

Lord Jesus, with us in his Holy Spirit, as he promised, to counsel, comfort and guide us in our struggles against persecution, until he returns to us to make all things new.

Amen! Come, Lord Jesus!

May the grace of our Lord Jesus Christ be with you all. Amen."

Part Two:
JOSEPH'S STORY

Joseph, a brother of Jesus, and son of Joseph the Carpenter

"Who is my mother? Who are my brothers?" : and looking round at them who were sitting in the circle about him he said "Here are my mother and brothers: whoever does the will of God is my brother, my sister and my mother."
(Mark's Gospel 3:vv33-35)

The morning sun threw soft shafts of silver light onto the range of tools, and through a fine cloud of wood shavings, that emitted a sweet aroma that mingled with the presence of animal droppings in our small house in Nazareth. A carpentry business.

My father was a working man, and a good man. Everyone in the village said so.

It wasn't hard to model myself on my father. The fact that he gave me the name echoing his filled me with a desire to follow in his shoes, and emulate his skills with wood.

My nose barely rose above the workbench as I watched Joseph handle tools with such intense precision, that shaved and smoothed the handle of a plough, or the leg of a bench. His dark hair, matted with sweat and sawdust, covered arms that rippled in tight cords where the muscles tightened – beard covered with dust and a face that spoke of deep, suppressed emotion. Those eyes, I remember even then, burned with a quiet conviction and something else that I later learned to be deep fathomed sorrow.

My mother was, of course, instructive and loving with a resolute firmness that matched her older husband. She had given birth to our elder brother when she was almost too young.

I, and my brothers, James, Jude and Simon knew that what we ever hoped to become would be modelled on the sheer magnitude of my father, the carpenter of Nazareth.

It was our older brother Yeshua I couldn't understand. Not for many years, anyway. He seemed set apart in so many disquieting ways. To my brothers and sisters, Yeshua –or Jesus as he became known, was a strong, kind and talented man.

'Yeshi' our little sisters called him.

What was almost incomprehensible was the way our father adopted a quite different tone of voice when speaking to our brother. Not so much respect as a form of communication that needed few words, accompanied by a deep look, exchanged between the old man and Yeshua.

There were times when, in the synagogue, my father would bow his head when Yeshua spoke to the Rabbi. My father the head of our family acting in this way!

With arms and head wound with phalacteri, Joseph and Yeshua intoned the scriptural responses and we all sang the Psalms and gave honour to Almighty God who had chosen us as His people. Watching through the grill that separated the women from the men our mother sat with our sisters, Susanna and Talitha.

The singing drifted out on the chill morning air, across the little houses and the animal paddocks. As we made our way out from worship we boys played and ran, and laughed. They were good times; hard, and often uncertain and filled with hunger, but good all the same. At the water well Yeshua once splashed us and our sisters and we responded.

This met with some hard glances from our elders in the village.

There was always work to be done, but not on the Sabbath; however, it *was* the Sabbath. Little did I realise at the time that our brother would one day cause an uproar on the Sabbath, and be driven out of the Synagogue just for quoting from the Prophet Isaiah.

In those early days Yeshua seemed so different, and acted in an increasingly distant way; he spent time away on his own, when not helping in the workshop.

One year there was a plague of locusts, and almost all the crops of the village were destroyed. Another time a drought, that seemed to go on for ever, and some of the sick and old died, as well as some animals. These were hard times. There were nights when my belly ached for want of water and food. But, through all these bad seasons Mother and Father remained strong, and gave us strength, so we didn't complain.

One night I rolled off my pallet, not able to sleep, and wanting to pass water. As I made my way back quietly, not wanting to disturb my parents, I heard a sound of a man's voice, and the sound of crying softly.

It was Yeshua. Standing in front of a field of ruined crops, arms outstretched, and tear stained face up to the sky.

As time went on we grew, and nothing much changed in Nazareth, except the increase in taxes imposed by the Romans. Along with the Denarii there was a Temple Tax, and too frequently our chickens, goats and even donkeys were taken if a householder found it difficult to pay. There was little mercy shown if a man complained or refused. We all hated the Tax Collectors, for they were Jews like us, in the pay of the Roman Governor.

I can still feel the sense of shame and anger as my brothers restrained me from speaking out impulsively. So, I kept my silence, as most of us did then.

But I knew there were some in the village who had sworn allegiance to the leaders of the Iscarii, young men who vowed to take down Roman oppression by force. Knives, sickles and swords were made and hidden in grain stores or buried in caves. They muttered angrily that one day our people would be free of domination.

James, Jude and Simon increased in their studies as I did, learning the Torah and both the Hebrew and Greek, as well as some Aramaic. We all saw less and less of Yeshua.

For days and even weeks we did not see him.

When he did appear he looked happy, but physically exhausted, but always had a kind word and a story for our young and excitable sisters. He seemed to lose weight after each time away, and our mother would set about trying to build him up again!

One day, at the time of the Feast of the Tabernacles, Yeshua brought a cousin home, called Johannes, or John. We all found this man really strange, wild and with a hard stare that was disturbing to us at the time. But he smiled when Talitha and Susanna held hands and danced around Yeshua with an old Hebrew song; one our father had told us had been sung by the children of the slaves when held captive by Pharaoh in Egypt, before Moses led the people out to find the Promised Land.

John spoke to us of the prophesies that told of the long awaited Messiah. Yeshua remained silent but looked intently at John. I noticed that my mother walked away, and covered her head, as if praying –or weeping.

THREE YEARS THAT CHANGED EVERYTHING

"....they were astonished, and said, ' Where did this man get this wisdom and these mighty Works? Is this not the carpenter's son? Is not his mother called Mary? Are not his brothers James and Joseph and Simon and Judas? And are not all his sisters with us?'.."(Matthew 13: 54b-56)

My first recollection of how much everything changed was when Yeshua brought home two friends, Andrew and his brother Cephas. Later he was given the name Peter, and he was in many ways the opposite of a rock, which the name meant; for Cephas seemed always to explode with some emotion or other, but we could see that our brother held him in deep affection.

My mother received the visitors with due hospitality, as was our custom. Susanna and Talitha helped serve food and drink, and had to interrupt the intense talk of young men, radiant with excitement and new vision.

Like my brothers, I was aware of the fishermen families, and especially Zebedee and his sons and stories circulated about their going out to catch fish on Lake Galilee where calm waters could change in minutes to wild waves and dangerous currents that capsized many a boat.

Andrew told us about the other men who now followed our brother. This news was strange to us, for why would they follow Yeshua at all?

Our mother sat with hands clasped to her face as Yeshua spoke of his baptism in the Jordan by his cousin. So many people had witnessed this, and our brother's face lit up with a new radiance I had not seen before.

If we had any doubts about where Yeshua had been prior to this then we were given the full story of his 'testing' as he called it, in the desert places. In fact, it seemed to us quite an exaggerated account, that brought up visions of an evil force trying to persuade him to come 'back to earth,' and find power through military might; it appeared that even the wild animals didn't threaten or harm him. Evidence of this ordeal showed in his sunburnt and thin body.

Rather than try to diffuse the flow of vibrant storytelling our two guests – whom Yeshua called his disciples – jumped in whenever there was a gap in our brother's story, to speak of how they had been called to follow him.

"Follow our brother?" James asked. "Where?"

It was then that we all began to see a change in Yeshua, and it was as if there was a veil between us and him.

He stood at the head of the table, and covered his head, and he seemed to grow in stature;

His voice became softer, but full of strong emotion as he looked down on each of us.

"Now is not the time to reveal all I have to say. Please let us enjoy this moment."

As the months and seasons came and went we saw less and less of him; but, all of us, at one time or another, sat and listened to him speak to great numbers of people of all ages.

Rumours of his arrival in a town or village spread like wildfire.

One particular memory was the day he spoke to a great number of people who had followed him all day. On arrival at a hillside overlooking the lake the crowds sat on the grass as Yeshua taught them about many new truths, and spoke of fulfilled prophesies.

As the day wore on there was a ripple of concern seemed to run through the listeners, as to where they were going to get food, for many of the families included children. Some of us had some unleavened bread and pouches with figs and a little wine, but many families had come unprepared.

Speaking with great clarity across the heads of the thousands of people, many physically worn out and very poor, or unwell, Yeshua talked about the Kingdom of God come among them – His people, as Yahweh had promised to the prophets long ago. This we all listened to with warmth and admiration, but a wave of muttering was heard from the crowds when our brother said the words, "My Father in Heaven."

One of his followers said to Yeshua that the people were hungry and asked how they could possibly feed so many? To this I saw our brother give a smile, and suggested that they, his chosen men, arrange to find food to go round. This was received by laughter.

Then in front of us a small boy rose and walked cautiously up to Yeshua, and held out some palm leaves in which lay some small loaves of bread and two small dried fish.

At this our brother did not smile, but knelt down and gently took the food offered by the small lad. Then he broke the bread into small fragments and also the fish and raised his hands in blessing to Yahweh.

Suddenly there were disciples moving among the people and handing out food; at the same time many produced whatever they had and began to share it with someone sitting next to them on the grass. But, the amazing thing was that baskets of food were left over and taken back to where our brother stood. Later, we learned there were about five thousand men, women and children who were fed that day.

There were numerous other occasions when food was shared, including a wedding in Cana, to which our mother had been invited to help organise the nuptials for the wedding feast.

Here, on this occasion of laughter and rejoicing the whole wedding party was in danger of finishing early as the wine ran out. James was there, and told us that there seemed to be a lot consumed by the guests; but, whatever the reason, Yeshua was asked by our mother to help to provide more wine. James was standing close by, and saw his brother was not pleased when asked to perform what amounted to a miracle of some sort.

But, however it happened, what was water became good wine, whole large jars of it of outstanding quality. Everyone had a marvellous time by all accounts. However, when myself, Jude and Simon sat together in the early evening a few days later, James seemed troubled about the whole miraculous occurrence at Cana. Our elder brother was beginning to attract attention from men of power and influence; and there were reports of threats against these 'miraculous' acts, of which there were many it seemed.

The following Summer Yeshua was away with his disciples, and we only heard news as it was brought back by other villagers, or travellers passing through Nazareth.

Someone had to run the family business, and carpentry was our trade. We began to resent our older brother's activities and the attention it brought. For not everyone was in love with Yeshua's teachings and healings, despite the fact that many witnesses came through villages and reported acts of healing; many people were given new sight, walked again, and were even cured of that horrifying disease, Leprosy, in all its forms. Anyone with that disease was banned from any community.

I became impatient to see and hear for myself the wonders of my brother, and despite James's scepticism I followed the disciples to the inside of Peter's house, where we sat in front of Yeshua as he spoke of the coming of a new order, that would bring hope and great prophetic wonders to the people of Israel.

While he was speaking there were noises in the roof, and slowly a ragged hole appeared.

Looking up we saw a man lying on a pallet being gently lowered by ropes to the earthen floor in front of Yeshua.

It was amazing and breathtaking to see a man lying curled and crippled, having been helped by four friends in desperation, and then to see this man slowly rise, and at Yeshua's command pick up his pallet and walk out of the house, followed by singing crowds!

We heard so many accounts of great and wonderful things in Judea; but, as enemies gathered like vultures, and the Pharisees and Sadducees united in opposition to this upstart village carpenter, creating unrest, we all felt great anxiety, and fear for both Yeshua and ourselves.

So, it was that our brother continued teaching and spread goodness, not unaware of the wave of hostility, but undeterred nonetheless. He remained primarily in Galilee until the feast of the Tabernacles in Jerusalem.

We brothers felt we needed to advise Yeshua to act more prudently, and felt that he should make more effort to win people over and confound his critics by displaying his good works more publicly. So we met with him, and advised him to go to Judea so that many more people would see him, and realise there was nothing to fear about rumours of his rabbinic ministry becoming out of hand, and putting him on a holy pedestal. We all knew what had happened to other young men of zeal who spoke of messianic fulfilment. Many were arrested and stoned to death. James was concerned about the attention drawn to not just our family but to our whole village, supposing that our taxes may be increased or something worse.

So we pleaded with Yeshua to go to Jerusalem and show himself to the people who needed to be persuaded that there would be no trouble and unrest.

In truth, at that time we all began to think our brother was becoming a little mad, and did find it increasingly hard to believe in him, as so many others clearly did.

Once again though, as before, he answered quietly, "My time is not yet come, but your time is always here." We did not understand these words, spoken as if he was detached and apart from us in some way – which in truth he was.

He sat down, and asked us to sit alongside him. "look my brothers", he said, looking at each of us in turn, "Go to the feast yourselves; I am not going up to this feast."

So, he remained in Galilee.

We didn't realise the depth of his thinking at the time, nor did we understand that he needed to move with some secrecy as there were threats that, unbelievably, men of our own faith and race were plotting to kill him.

Later, about the middle of the festival we heard our brother had arrived and was in the great temple. I saw him myself sitting on steps in a portico surrounded by learned men who had been drawn by the sound of Yeshua's voice as the way he spoke with great depth and insight about the prophesies being fulfilled. As I quietly moved forward enough to hear, without attracting attention, I saw many men in robes that showed their priestly authority and young students of the Law. They had evidently been listening for several hours, and although one or two drifted away talking quietly, and glancing back in evident hostility, most just listened attentively. Then, there was a pause, and, as any rabbi was accustomed to do, our brother paused for questions. At first there was just astonishment at the depth of his knowledge of scripture and Mosaic laws; but then a Pharisee asked where this young man had received teaching to speak with such confidence and skill?

Our brother's answer began calmly enough, relating all authority to Yahweh and that it was available to anyone to discern whether his teaching was from God or just from his own experience and opinion.

I wanted to find my brothers, but I was afraid for Yeshua, as I could overhear men on the fringes of the audience declare that our brother had no authority, and were very rude and disdainful about the fact that we were a simple working family from a poor community, and that Yeshua was only the son of a carpenter. Also it was generally accepted that there was no prophet to have come out of Galilee,

It was then that we had the first clear indication that things were becoming dangerous for my brother, and anyone who kept company with him. for, the moment when he stood and very loudly cried out,

"The one who sent me is true, and you do not know him, and I know him because I am from him,.....and he sent me!"

anger erupted, and men were throwing sandals and shouting, and one scribe tore his robes. Someone called for the temple police to make an arrest for blasphemy.

He walked quickly away, surrounded and shielded by some of his closest disciples.

As the great festival drew to a close we were ready to head for home, but went to find our brother and persuade him to travel with us back to Nazareth. It was the last day when James and I found him. His whole manner had changed from quiet scholarly talk to loud but confident preaching.

Clearly a large crowd were impressed and excited by what he said, but to us he seemed to speak in a way that was confusing, and full of great imagery .

"Out of the believer's heart, "he called out, "shall flow rivers of living water."

If it were just that our brother risked being arrested or harmed in any way it would be bad enough, but as the days moved on Yeshua seemed to attract both admirers and enemies alike. His very acts of kindness, compassion and amazing acts of healing produced more and more a frenzy of distrust, especially among the elite who feared the condemnation of the Romans.

Take the incidence of the time he was disturbed in the Temple Courts at Jerusalem. In the midst of a long teaching session men who called themselves the true 'Teachers of the Law' dragged a woman who it was claimed had been caught in the act of adultery. The clear punishment for this was death by stoning. Nobody asked where the man was who carried out the other part of the sexual act, as our custom is always to protect the male.

Apparently, so we were informed, there were a group of men who were desperately trying to trap our brother and have him arrested for breaking the law or condoning lawlessness.

It was clear, according to our sources, that this was a major incident, as even our brother's words to the accusers sped around the villages later.

He is reported to have said

"If anyone is without sin, let him be the first to throw a stone at her!" Stones were hurled down in the dust and angry plotters turned away and stalked off plotting revenge for this humiliation.

Our mother, Mary, spoke to this woman some days later, and her whole life was renewed, and whilst finding it hard to being accepted back in the community, she was welcomed into our home where she told us that our brother had forgiven her, and she promised to sin no more.

But, we muttered amongst ourselves. How could Yeshua forgive sins? Who was he claiming to be? The rumours upset all of us, especially our sisters, for we all loved Yeshua; called Jesus, as many saw him as a Saviour.

Were the rumours true......that this, our flesh and blood brother was the Promised One, the Messiah? It seemed too frightening to be true, because we all knew what had happened to other men who had made such claims. Also, surely, we all said, the Messiah would come with a great military force and drive out the Romans and make Israel victorious?

I was impressed by one of our brother's followers, a man the others trusted to hold the purse in order that they could find the most basic food and drink. This young man, one Judas Iscariot, seemed quite different from the other eleven specially chosen men; but it was his passionate attempts to convince the others about the need for Yeshua to use greater force and power against Rome and the ruling authorities that impressed me. It sounded a very sensible and wise line of thinking. When I talked about this to my brothers they all agreed that Yeshua was taking too soft a line altogether. Forgiveness and compassion had their place, of course, as the Holy Scripture of the Talmud taught, but without an army or military might, how could our brother hope to see the reality of the Kingdom he talked so much about?

These were worrying days.

As news of each healing miracle reached us, we were increasingly alarmed. Of course it was wonderful that a blind man now had his sight, and people who were crippled and hideously deformed walked straight backed, and laughed and sang, praising our God! Yes, we shared the excitement of the vast numbers of people who flocked to see, and hear our brother, but couldn't hide our misgivings from Yeshua; so much so that he spent little time amongst his family.

By now all the stories about him had become so familiar, that men began to memorize these acts in verse and song, like the blessed Psalms. On the rare occasions when we stood apart listening and watching we saw a young man writing on a wax tablet or a piece of pottery, so presumably recording some of our brother's sayings and parables.

Little did we know just how important these records would become.

DARKENING SKIES

It was when a close friend of Yeshua, Lazarus was brought back to life that any hope of the enemies of our brother and his followers quietly dismissing his activities as harmless then disappeared; hostility grew like a menacing, dark shadow, and we were all very fearful of repercussions from the authorities.

We knew of his friendship with Lazarus and his sisters, Mary and Martha in Bethany; he would stay with them on occasions and rest.

Our brother had been away during the winter months at the Feast of Dedication, and it was there that many scribes and Pharisees gathered like vultures – throwing question after question in order to trick him in some way that would gain witnesses to accuse him of the sin of blasphemy. By that time the knives were out, and his hecklers used words like "the Christ" to get Yeshua to declare once and for all who he claimed to be.

So many times men took up stones to hurl at his head, but each time he asked them, 'Of which sin was he to blame? Were they condemning him because of the acts of healing they had witnessed? There was so much anger on one side, and such praise and admiration by the vast majority, so no stoning took place.

Yeshua went back to the place where he had been baptised by his cousin, John. This great Firebrand and wild man, with a reputation known by all as a prophet, had been beheaded.

So at the Jordan Jesus continued teaching, and there he heard of Lazarus and how close to death he was. He was followed by so many people at the time that we began to wonder to ourselves what it was that made him so special and adored by so many. We had not grasped the importance of what this whole period of our brother's life was about.

When news came that Lazarus had died he did not hurry, but slowly made his way to Bethany, to be confronted by Mary and Martha, and wailing women surrounding the tomb where Lazarus had been laid after embalming several days before.

We were not present, but what happened defied all logic. Lazarus came out of the tomb, freed from the cloth that had bound him, at a loud command from Yeshua.

Rather than convince the cynics and opponents of his teaching, this incredible miracle, for that is undeniably what it was, made many converts but filled his enemies with hate.

After these incredible events an invisible net seemed to close around anyone who was associated with our brother and his disciples. Crowds continued to run to hear him speak and as a family we no longer kept up with all the adulation and excitement. There was work to do, and in any case we wanted to keep our heads down so as not to attract attention.

What really put the cat among the pigeons was the entrance into Jerusalem on a mule, with huge crowds, children among them, shouting 'Hosanna to the son of David' and waving palm branches. In some ways we were not surprised at such a public display of support for our brother, as Judas had told us that something like this needed to happen to stimulate the people into greater support of this cause that would overthrow the oppressors. In among the singing people along the road, men with hidden daggers concealed in their cloaks walked, awaiting any opportunity to strike at the Roman soldiers who were watching from a safe distance. Among them was their leader, Judas had told us about, Bar-Abbas.

This in itself was a flagrant act of defiance, and the Temple leaders commanded that Yeshua stop the procession and the singing and send the people home, as this was attracting too much negative attention.

But, when our brother entered the Holy City and walked up the Temple steps he was shocked to see men buying and selling, and money changers doing deals and shouting to attract attention. Nobody was prepared for what happened next. Yeshua began turning over the tables, releasing the caged birds, and then proceeded to raise a knotted rope above his head and drove the screaming stallholders out, shouting that this should be a house of prayer, but they had turned it into a den of corruption and a violation against Yahweh.

What I then heard later was a collation of reports passed on to us, through James. At the time of the Passover when we were gathered around our own table in Nazareth, Yeshua had asked that his closest followers met in an upper room. Only much later have we heard the details of this meal. At the time we were naturally envious of an especially selected group who seemed to be closer than his own kith and kin. We all recalled the time he asked aloud

'Who is my mother? Who are my brothers?' and felt so rejected and humiliated. Little did we comprehend the depth of meaning that our brother gave to all his public statements. It became so clear as the terrible events rushed upon Yeshua like a pack of wolves, that he not only professed but lived a life of love for everyone, even his enemies. Shortly after that meal, when Yeshua was praying with his disciples in the Garden of Gethsemane, Judas, the same one we had admired so much, betrayed him with a kiss that acted as a signal for the temple guards to arrest him and drag him away. We always asked why Peter and Andrew or James and John did not fight for him or plead his innocence.

Would we, his family, have acted like them and done nothing? Surely not!

So began a rapid series of accusations before the Sanhedrin, Herod and finally Pontius Pilate who as Procurator held the fate of every man, Jew especially, in his hands. At that stage we, his brothers and our mother and sisters were barely able to understand what was being said or what decisions were made, as we were right at the back of the crowds, and covering our faces in case we were recognised and arrested. I remember, though, that Mary, our mother refused to cover her face, and just stood with her eyes closed, white with an inner agony we could barely imagine at the time. All she said, as it became evident that the howling mobs had persuaded Pilate not to free our brother was,

"My son. My dear son."

We were anxious to get away, as we heard the dreadful sound of "Crucify him!" and we cried tears of grief but also of terror; the sort of terror that can drive the bravest of men to their knees. We saw our brother come into view carrying the cross bar that would be the base on which he would be hung. Soldiers pushed him on and held back the crowd, where one woman, that Mary of Magdala whom we had met after her forgiveness by Yeshua sobbed and called out the words

"Master" and "Lord."

None of the disciples could be seen, except John, the youngest, who suddenly appeared and took our mother's arm, covered her head and led her away.

This was our chance, and we ran as fast as we could and away from that terrifying scene.

What was this madness, we called out to each other, that drove our brother to bring such destruction to himself, and humiliation to his friends and family?

So, we – like many others, ran away and hid, for fear of reprisals by Roman Legions against our villages.

Through that long night, the darkness was enveloping us all, and the whole world it seemed, and I wanted to cry, and could only hide and keep silent.

Then one of our villagers came and told us that he had been in the vicinity of the killing of our brother, and that there were two other men crucified on either side of him on the Hill of the Skull. He and several others, slow to leave, were ordered to clean up the route where there was evidence on the blood stained ground from the Via Dolorosa to the hill at Golgotha.

This man, with a wildness and fear in his face, but a strange, distant look in his eyes, told us that John had taken our mother home with him, after they and other women helped to lower the broken body of Yeshua from his place of execution. According to this neighbour our brother had called out some words

"Father, into your hands" .....but the rest was swept away by the wind that had begun to rage across the hilltop.

"Father?" he said. "Do you think he was talking to your later and honourable father, Joseph?"

None of us answered. Our thoughts disturbed us greatly. It had already begun to dawn on us that there had happened something that defied all logic and reality, and that in that cry from the cross came the realization that our brother was crying out to God..........and calling *Him* 'Father!'

We had to remain in hiding and wait for the morning to come, and for things to quieten down. There would be the burial to arrange, but maybe this could be arranged somewhere inconspicuous, so that things would get back to the way they were, before this devastating series of events that began so quietly three years before.

A NEW DAWN

Our perception of exactly what happened after our brother was taken down from the cross and buried was clouded by fear; we were enveloped by a mood of uncertainty but also impatience to know what the future held for us all.

Joseph of Arimathea, prominent and influential, respected by the Sanhedrin, gave permission for Yeshua's body to be entombed. As was the custom, the body was washed by the women, and spices and perfumes anointed the shroud cloth that covered our beloved brother.

At Herod's orders a huge stone was rolled over the entrance, sealing it, and guards were posted.

Of course, all of us were not at the tomb. Our mother was staying with the disciple John, and we tried to escape attention by waiting at home in Nazareth. We awaited the retribution that would surely fall on all of us, and many more across the hills and into Jerusalem. There was work to be done come daylight and we set to and worked frenetically for the next two days. Mother came with John and led us in prayers at mealtimes, and at night we lit candles to remind ourselves of the light that had been snuffed out with our brother's execution. We also sang Psalms, quietly so as not to draw attention to ourselves.

Jude said on one occasion,

"Yeshua is out of all harm and danger, now."

James prayed that our brother's soul would find rest in the peace of Yahweh, who would surely send another messiah to free our people?

We knew that we were to fulfil the days of mourning required by custom, but to our great amazement Mary kept reassuring us with prayers of hope, saying that if we waited, very soon something good would come out of this time of grief and shock.

None of us could understand, and felt that our mother was showing false optimism for all our benefits.

We were told that the eleven disciples were hiding somewhere, as Matthew came to tell us about the death of Judas Iscariot, who had taken his own life. If it was true that this young man whom we thought we knew betrayed Yeshua, then it was clear that he could not live with himself. Money had been found scattered at the base of the tree below his corpse, so clearly he had been well paid by the authorities.

On the dawn of the third day after Yeshua's burial I walked alone outside and looked across the village as the rising sun touched the rooftops, and on across the animals grazing on the hillsides. There was no breeze, and it was going to be another hot day, but a strange light was filling the sky, and it became hard to see without being blinded.

Mother was going back with John that morning, and made us a meal that we would all share before her departure. We lay around the small table and dipped pieces of unleavened bread in olive oil, and handed round a bowl of figs and pieces of fish.

Outside there were sounds of activity in the village as another working day began. Women walked to the well, some carrying small children, and men set about their work, as our old donkey pawed impatiently at the dry ground. We began to gather our tools, ready to set to work.

I looked up at a wooden yoke, fitted for two oxen, and recalled that Yeshua had crafted that with hands that became rough and strong like our father, Joseph. I then remembered that he told us once a parable about those beasts of burden, working as a pair, but the lead oxen was the one who controlled the direction. He then spoke of this in a way in which he would always be the source of strength whatever happened to us; I didn't realise at the time how much stronger he was than us, not physically, but with an inner strength which drew on the strength he found from spending time in Prayer to Yahweh. Now, as I looked at the oxen yoke I realised that it was shaped like a wooden cross. I shuddered, and felt that I needed Yeshua's strength more than anything else.

Suddenly, there was a shout, and it was our mother calling. We thought she had left the village but here she was laughing and clapping her hands. Talitha and Susanna were crying, but dancing around their mother when we ran up to her. We recognised James, Zebedee's Son, one of the disciples of Yeshua, and listened in amazement as he breathlessly told us of the miracle that had taken place! Mary of Magdala had gone to the tomb and found it empty! Possibly some group of men had pushed back the stone after overpowering the sentries and taken the body away, as she thought at first.

She then spoke to a man who she thought was the cemetery gardener, and that man she spoke to was our brother, Yeshua!

He said to her, "Mary".

He actually spoke. It was our brother, and he was alive again.

Mary ran and told the disciples and Peter and John ran to the empty tomb and saw for themselves, but could not understand. On their return there was confusion, and Thomas declared himself not prepared to believe anything unless he saw for himself the wounds that had made great marks in our brother's hands and feet.

You can imagine how our reactions were a mixture of wonder, huge happiness, and at the same time an element of disquiet. We were very troubled, and James, Jude and Simon and I all exchanged looks that clearly showed our guilt at having doubted Yeshua. When I think of the way we thought him deranged and dangerously self deluding!

Whatever happened now we were certain that nothing would ever be the same again.

It wasn't long before we heard that Yeshua had appeared to his disciples and Thomas had reached out and touched the marks of our brother's wounds. Yet, we were told, he was changed in a way that was so difficult to describe.

We had to be patient, yet all the time we were anxious to see for ourselves the man who shared our kinship, but had a part of him that was from the Heavenly Father, Yahweh, as the prophets had written in so many places in Holy Scripture.

All the faithful people had called him Jesus. It seemed that our faith had been shallow.

One day we were all emerging from the synagogue on the Sabbath, and as Law directed we did not work, but spent the day in quiet, and prayer. Sadly, the rabbi had not made any mention of what had happened, except to say that one of our number, the eldest son of Mary and the late Joseph had been killed by the Romans for claiming to be the Messiah and inciting unrest among the people. The old man chose his words carefully, and I could see he was afraid that he might say something that would be blasphemous. The other men who sat with us, heads covered did not meet our eyes or speak when we left the synagogue except to mutter words of commiseration.

As we sat in our homes, for two of us, myself and Jude had taken wives from among the women in the village, we awaited any news that would bring us to a place where our dear brother might appear, as he had done to a chosen few.

James had gone up to Jerusalem, for he was becoming a respected member of the Temple community.

Simon was considering training to be a Rabbi, and was under the tutorship of a respected Teacher of the Law. But, I could see that he was in two minds whether to continue as the whole question of where our people were being led had been turned upside down by the Ministry, and subsequent Resurrection of Jesus.

All of us were compiling our own memories of what our brother had said and done through three turbulent years. As we compared notes each time we met we were excited about the clear similarities in our writings. Although we were naturally using different memories that were important to each of us, we agreed on so many wonderful acts of healing, teaching and, above all, his quiet compassion.

"Yes" one of us would say, "Remember that time he brought back to life the little daughter of Jairus...................and that day that a man with a withered hand was healed?" So many memories came flooding in, along with the huge number of reports from those who had been with Yeshua when we were not.

At that time, as we sat comparing stories and notes, I wondered if any of the disciples would be skilled enough to put these miracles and happenings in some sort of order so it could be shared? Perhaps one of the followers, Matthew perhaps, would find a way to pass on the good news. It would take some considerable skill to separate fact from rumours.

Who would write what had happened that terrible day of the crucifixion, as we had not been there? The guilt of that alone was enough to drive us to despair. Would it be John? Both he and my mother had witnessed the torture and agony of Yeshua. What about the young man, we knew as Markus who had followed wherever our brother went, and who had become a disciple to Peter? We knew that he had been observing and possibly writing what he saw with his own eyes.

But, he couldn't speak of what we knew- our brother's early years with us as a family. He wouldn't know anything of the events of Yeshua's birth in Bethlehem in Judea, and what we knew had been told to us by our mother, Mary.

Yes, we all had opinions and memories, and views which we wanted to share with others.

However, it was still dangerous to make public these views, and so we met in secret and talked quietly among ourselves, and those we could trust not to betray us to the Romans.

So the days moved to weeks, and there was still so much that we could only hear from the eleven remaining men of the original twelve Yeshua, or Jesus, had called.

It seemed hard to believe that we, his brothers, could not be privileged to be invited to places where Jesus appeared. A couple had met and walked with him, and eaten a meal; several hundred claimed to have been aware of his presence, not to touch him, but to know it was Jesus, real but yet unreal. Transformed, but clear to see as a man.

Then one incredible moment our anxieties were stilled, and our hopes fulfilled. Jesus had appeared to my brother, James. He had been praying in Jerusalem, and there was my brother, kneeling by his side, and praying with him!

I could not understand why James had been so chosen, but his request was answered, as on an evening when we were all seated at a table, our sisters included, there was a great light that shone so brightly as to cause us to cover our eyes, and there was Jesus standing at head of the table. Mary, our mother was with us, as she had been suffering for several days and John had brought her to be with us at this time, which was a great comfort to us all.

Our brother – and it was certainly he, although strangely different in a way that defies all description – placed a hand on the head of our mother, but did not speak. His eyes shone, with a power that only comes from a deep sense of personal love, and he looked at each of us in turn, holding our gaze. I wanted to drop my eyes, and yet his look penetrated my whole body. I remembered the story of the oxen and the yoke, and tears welled up.

Then just five words, said in a voice that sounded like music.

"My peace I give you."

Then he was gone. There was birdsong. The sound of chickens scratching.

How long we sat there I cannot remember, but none of us said a word. But, when I looked at Mary

I saw a light in her lined and tired eyes that seemed to give her a radiance, and we knew that, whatever happened to us in future this special moment gave us all a feeling that all would be well.

That moment, that very long moment, was able to prepare us for what happened next, on the day of Pentecost.

We had all gone into Jerusalem, because we were told that the Eleven had called for a new Disciple to replace Judas Iscariot. There had been a choice between a man with my name, -one Joseph, also called Bar-Sabbas, and Matthias, who was clearly held in high regard, for he was chosen after a time of prayer. Matthias joined the many others who came together on the day of Pentecost, and we were so fortunate to be among so many.

Without any warning a violent wind swirled around us, and we sat still, afraid that there might be a sudden storm. It seems almost impossible to fully describe – but what appeared like tongues of fire seemed to descend on each of our heads. As a man we rose to our feet, and a power that could only be Divine filled us. We felt our lungs would burst, and began to talk, and then sing, and look at each other with new eyes. It was as if the very Spirit of Yahweh had drawn out our breath, and replaced each one of us with new breath, and a sense of excitement mingled with great happiness.

These were men of different dialects and foreign languages, who, amazingly had been united in a way that swept all language barrier away. A man next to me, clearly an Egyptian spoke and I understood him.

We were like men who had taken too much wine, and raised our hands and called out to each other in ecstasy. The fact that we were drawing attention to ourselves, and that the Temple police and the Roman guards began to appear did not dilute this incredible feeling of liberation. Nine in the morning and we were revelling like men at sunset at a wedding!

Cephas, now Peter, who was clearly accepted as the leader among the disciples began to speak, loudly at first, and then, as we turned and quietly listened to him. He explained to all who could hear that we were not intoxicated by wine, but by the fulfilment of the prophets, and he quoted from the prophet Joel. It was the word 'Spirit' that made us all stop and listen.

"In the last days, God declares, I will pour out my Spirit upon all flesh..........................."

So Peter spoke with a sense of authority we had never heard before. What was especially shocking to our ears was the statement that *we had all* been responsible for the crucifixion of Jesus. My brothers and I understood what it cost Peter to say this, as he had not been able to remain loyal to his Master at the time of his arrest and trial.

As men drew around him, as much as in protection as anything else, Peter began to warm to his address, and took the huge number of men from all nationalities and languages back to the roots of our ancestry, in David, warrior and divinely appointed king. From this line came the line that, at the appointed time, brought the long-awaited Messiah.

Then came a call to the word metanoia, 'repent.'

There were cries of 'Baptism' and we all began to move out of the city to the banks of the Jordan, and it is reported that over three thousand men and women were baptised with water and the Spirit by the disciples.

For James, Jude, Simon and myself this was a momentous time. So often we had ridiculed and doubted the sanity of our elder brother. We had been in fear of our own safety, and even concerned about our family honour. Now, we were changed men. Indeed our sisters also had no difficulty in accepting the incredible happenings. In truth, I suspected that they had trusted and believed long before we, his brothers, had.

So, we also joined the three thousand and went down into the water to be baptised.

What happened over the next few days was astounding. Despite all the rumours of severe punishment for anyone who appeared to cause unrest, families were sharing their food and possessions with anyone in each part of their own community who was in need. Men who had not spoken to their neighbour for years opened their doors and bread was broken around family tables. At each meal prayers were spoken by the head of the host family and the name of Jesus the Messiah was called out, and the word 'Christos' was said. Psalms were sung and everyone embraced and exchanged a kiss of peace.

It became clear that this was an unstoppable force, and men spoke of taking the good news of what had happened to towns and villages far from Judea.

Our mother, Mary accompanied by John and Talitha, my little sister, made plans to go to Ephesus in the future, but in the meantime John worked closely with Peter. For myself, Jude and Simon, we could either return to Nazareth, or work with James in Jerusalem, although we all knew there was the possibility of arrest and torture, and even death.

Before we parted we shared a meal once more and renewed our commitment to tell others about the incredible miracles and teachings of our brother Jesus, and above all his still quite breathtakingly wonderful return to life from the tomb.

NEW DANGERS AND A NEW DISCIPLE

After some of the family went to Ephesus and close friends who had become believers and followers of The Way left the familiar homes in Galilee, we began to meet secretly in places unknown to the Romans and the Sanhedrin. Every day one of our number was arrested, but often released after a flogging. Secret tunnels, catacombs, were extended below the Holy City and throughout Judea, and as time went on men and women died and were buried in these secret places.

The disciples who were still led by Peter directed us in the way of sharing bread and wine, and using special prayers in remembrance of Jesus. Peter and John were often seen moving among the sick and disabled, showing compassion, and there were healings reported.

But, new dangers came to remove our spiritual leaders as Peter and John were thrown into prison. Miraculously they were set free, and went to preach in the temple; they were brought before the High Priest and allowed to speak about their faith and accused the priesthood of murdering Jesus. Judas, and Simon and I were witnesses to this hearing and expected our leaders to be put to death.

Amazingly one of the respected Pharisees of the Council, Gamaliel appealed for calm and suggested that they might become martyrs and create more trouble. So they were freed!

Not content with this pardon, despite being warned not to speak the name of Jesus, you will not be surprised to know that Peter and John did exactly that!

We seemed an unstoppable army of followers. The disciples were exhausted as they all welcomed increasing numbers and spent days and nights in people's homes teaching and healing.

Our little carpentry business was barely managed, but manage we did, as apprentices among the faithful offered their skills in working with wood. We would all have liked to have been given special positions alongside the main disciples but were happy to be a part of this great movement.

Little did we realise that such enthusiasm would create a new wave of opposition and so many enemies who wanted to stop us all from speaking out or saying anything where the name of Jesus was spoken.

Peter declared that a special group of men were needed to work for the Disciples, and seven men from among the Greek followers of The Way were given special duties after a selection was made to find men deeply spiritual and deemed wise among their peers. These seven men named Philip, Prochorus, Nicanor,

Timon, Parmenas and Nichlaus, were joined with a young, zealous man called Stephen.

All of us were present when we gathered in a secret place and the senior disciples or Apostles prayed and laid hands on the seven.

The effect of building a multi-layered team had great effect on the evangelical work as so many more men and women became disciples, including some of the temple priests! Stephen's personality and gifts were such that it brought him into conflict with a variety of men in the communities in Judea. Men from the Synagogue of the Freedmen, which included people who were residents of Alexandria and parts of Asia plotted to bring Stephen down, with charges of blasphemy. For all of us, we could see that the same false charges that had been levelled against Jesus were being used as weapons to bring down followers of Christ. So, it happened that whilst speaking crowds turned on Stephen and stoned him to death.

We were devastated, and feared once more for our lives and all our families.

Yet, out of this crisis arose the most unlikely champion of all we believed and had sworn to follow.

Saul of Tarsus was a man with a mission that gave him authority to hunt down the faithful, even breaking into their homes with armed men and throwing great numbers into prison. This same man, learned yet fanatical in his obsession to drive out all believers of the church actually stood to witness the stoning of Stephen – and yet, as witnesses have testified who were with him when he was blinded whilst travelling to Damascus he suddenly changed.

The man who had made it his mission to imprison and torture the followers of Jesus became in his dramatic conversion an ambassador for our risen and triumphant brother. With his new name, Paul, he was- despite misgivings and opposition initially from Peter- accepted as an Apostle and began to journey far from Judea, and into Samaria, where Philip had been before him. In time his letters to churches across Galatia and into Corinth in Greece before travelling to Rome under arrest became circulated, and we were encouraged and driven on ourselves.

These were increasingly dangerous times for all followers of The Way. Men and women were arrested and beheaded or crucified or humiliated in front of Roman nobility, and it became more and more risky to state openly our belief.

Tragically my brother James, whilst holding a position of great respect among the leaders in Jerusalem was arrested and put to the sword. When

I think of how much we all used to scoff and deride Yeshua, and thought him insane, James most of all it is almost beyond any belief that we became disciples of our wonderful brother. A man who was one of us, a member of our family, headed by our loving parents Joseph and Mary; a man who shared our meals, our lives, who laughed and played and sang songs of great beauty. This, our brother was more than just a man from Galilee – *is* so much more.

We all had a new sense of purpose now, and wherever we found safety to live, some of us will marry and raise families, who will carry on our line through future generations. People will know of the great wonder of Christ Jesus, and I am convinced that disciples will travel to all parts of the world, just as Paul is doing now, and even if it means suffering and worse our future generations will tell the stories.

Simon, Jude, and my sisters - we all mourn the death of James, and yet, because of what has happened we do not feel sad, but elated and inextricably bonded together forever.

This morning, as the sun rose quickly above the hills I closed our little carpenters shop in Nazareth. I looked around at the tools, the workbench, and especially the wooden yoke hanging over the door, and felt deep emotion for the things of childhood.

There was my father, hands blistered and gnarled, and Yeshua holding a length of new wood about to be planed. There were the girls, giggling and running after my mother to the well to draw water. There were my brothers, Simon, Jude and James, talking and laughing.

My wife, Rebekka was with child, and we are travelling out of Judea to a place of safety. But we will return. This is our land. The land of our forefathers The land that brought our people, chosen by Yahweh, in which was contained the line of David, that came down through the generations to where our specially chosen brother was to become not just the new head of the family line, but a whole new beginning for all of us.

About the Author

After a lifetime of serving Christ through church, mission, hospital, and Prayerline but working in those fields in their individual ways, the Reverend Norman and Mrs. Barbara Setchell use their experiences to provide a fictional story providing insight into Jesus's life. With the Bible as a canvas, they create a unique portrayal of the life of Jesus as seen through the eyes of two of His siblings.

Printed in Great Britain
by Amazon.co.uk, Ltd.,
Marston Gate.